THIS BLOOMSBURY BOOK

BELONGS TO

....

For my family - AS

BLOOMSBURY
CHILDREN'S
BOOKS

First published in Great Britain in 2005 by Bloomsbury Publishing Plc
38 Soho Square, London, W1D 3HB

Copyright © Adam Stower 2005
The moral right of the author/illustrator has been asserted

A CIP catalogue record of this book is available from the British Library
ISBN 0 7475 7550 9

Designed by Sarah Hodder

Printed and bound in China by South China Printing Co.

1 3 5 7 9 10 8 6 4 2

All papers used by Bloomsbury Publishing are natural, recyclable products made from wood
grown in well-managed forests. The manufacturing processes conform to the environmental
regulations of the country of origin.

The Den

Adam Stower

BLOOMSBURY
CHILDREN'S
BOOKS

Moving into a new home is hard work.
Rabbit tried his best to help, but Mum seemed to
think she could manage very well without him.

'Why not go out and make yourself a new friend?'
she said eventually. 'Just come back in time for tea.'

Rabbit hadn't been exploring for long when a big, bright blue ball came bouncing down the dusty road towards him.

'Where there's a ball, there are friends to be made,' he thought excitedly, grabbing the ball tightly with both paws.

And sure enough,
a pig came trotting
up to Rabbit.

'Hello,' said Rabbit, smiling his friendliest smile.
'That,' said Pig very loudly, 'is MY ball!'
And, snatching it away from Rabbit, he waddled
away quickly the way he had come.

'Well, that's not very friendly,' thought Rabbit. 'If he won't be my friend, I'll make my own friend to play with, just like Mum said.'

So Rabbit fetched some paper and his pencils and drew up a Plan.

Then he went to look for all of the things he might need.

When everything was ready, Rabbit began to make his friend. He was getting on well when once again Pig's ball was kicked towards him. This time it was Dog who fetched it.

'Hello, what are you doing?' Dog asked curiously.
'I'm making a friend to play with,' replied Rabbit.
'If you put a door on it that would make a great den!'
said Dog, throwing the ball back to the others.
'Come with me!'

'This will be perfect,' said Rabbit,
as he and Dog ran back to the den.

They were followed by Mouse and Tortoise who wanted to see what all the excitement was about.

'If that's a den you're building, then you'll be needing my tools,' grinned Tortoise. 'And some windows,' added Mouse, 'and Squirrel's got some paint!'

So Rabbit, Dog, Tortoise, Mouse and Squirrel all set off
to search for everything they might need for their den.

And Rabbit knew just the place to go.

Meanwhile, it was Pig who was
left feeling lonely.
He felt bad about being rude to Rabbit
and now he thought hard of how he
could make it up to him.
He thought of just the thing.

'Will this be of any use?' Pig asked.
'Oh, thanks, Pig. That's just the finishing touch we need,'
Rabbit smiled.

At last, as the sun sank below the trees,
the den was complete.

Everyone stood back to admire their hard work.
But, just then, the den creaked a little.
Then it creaked a lot.
Then it swayed and shuddered …

… and then it came CRASHING down!

As the dust cleared, the den lay in ruins.
Rabbit was very upset.
'Never mind, Rabbit,' said Pig. 'We can build a better
one tomorrow!'

And they all went home for tea, already dreaming
of the new den they were going to build together …